# Skipper Is the Daddy

## by Yoko Imoto

*American text by Margo Lundell*

GROSSET & DUNLAP · *New York*

Originally published as BOKUWA OTOUSAN by Yoko Imoto. Copyright © 1982 by Yoko Imoto.
American translation rights arranged with KIN-NO-HOSHI CO., LTD.,
Tokyo through Japan Foreign-Rights Centre. Translation copyright © 1989 by Grosset & Dunlap, Inc.
All rights reserved. First published in the U.S.A. in 1989 by Grosset & Dunlap, Inc., a member of
The Putnam Publishing Group, New York. Published simultaneously in Canada. Printed in Hong Kong.
Library of Congress Catalog Card Number: 88-81253    ISBN 0-448-09294-8
A B C D E F G H I J

One quiet Saturday morning Skipper Kitten stops playing and looks at his dad. Skipper is thinking about something.

Finally he says, "You're lucky, Daddy."

"Why do you say that, Son?" asks Dad.

"Because," says Skipper, "you get to drink coffee and stay up late—and never take naps!"

Dad laughs. "But Skipper," he says, "I *like* to take naps."

"Then you should be the son," says Skipper.

"And who will be the daddy?" asks Dad.

"I will!" says Skipper.

Dad thinks about this plan.

Then he says, "All right, Skipper. I'll be the son for today, and you can be the daddy."

"Hooray!" cries Skipper, jumping up and down.

Skipper puts on his dad's big hat and tie.
He finds some old glasses to wear. Then he
looks at himself in the mirror. He likes the
way he looks.

"Now I'm the daddy!" says Skipper.

*Clomp, clomp. Clomp, clomp.*

Mom hears Skipper walking down the hall in Dad's big shoes.

"Excuse me," says Skipper in a deep voice. "I'm very busy. I have to go read the newspaper."

For a while everything is just fine. The little daddy reads his newspaper. The big son reads a storybook.

Then Skipper's mom comes into the room.
"Oh, dear," she says. "This stool has a
wobbly leg and I can't fix it."
"That's a job for Daddy," says Skipper.

"Yes," says Dad. "And who's the daddy?"
"I am!" Skipper cries.

So Skipper gets out his daddy's tools. He tries to fix the wobbly leg.

"This is hard work," says the little daddy.

"I'm working hard, too," says the big son.

Before long Skipper is hot and tired. And the wobbly leg has wobbled right off the stool!

"I don't know how to fix this," sighs Skipper.

"Never mind," says Mom to the little daddy. "You can work on this broken clock instead."

"I'm working on this doughnut," says the big son.

Skipper tries his best to fix the clock.
He takes it apart, but then he can't
put it back together.

"Great Cats!" cries Skipper angrily.
"I don't know how to fix this clock either!"

"It's time for someone to take a nap," says Mom.
"That's me," says Dad.

When the big son is asleep,
Mom gets ready to go out.
"I'm going to the store now,"
she tells the little daddy. "Look
after things while I am gone."

But Skipper doesn't know how to look after things!
He feels scared and lonely with his mom away and his
dad asleep.

"Wake up, Dad! Wake up!" he cries. "I don't want
to be the daddy anymore!"

"All right, Skipper," says Dad. "I'll be the daddy again."

Now Skipper feels much better. He lies down to rest.

Soon Mom comes home. In her hand is a red box tied with pink string.

"Here's something special for Daddy!" she calls.

"I'll take care of that," says Dad. "I'm the daddy now."
"No! No!" cries Skipper. "I'm the daddy for today!"
So Mom gives the red box to Skipper . . .

And this time the little daddy knows just what to do!